Weekly Reader Books Presents

MORRIS
THE MOOSE

An Early I Can Read Book®

by B. Wiseman

HARPER & ROW, PUBLISHERS

Published by arrangement with Harper & Row,
Publishers, Inc. Weekly Reader is a federally registered
trademark of Field Publications. Early I Can Read Book
is a registered trademark of Harper & Row, Publishers, Inc.

Morris the Moose
Copyright © 1959, 1989 by Bernard Wiseman
Printed in the U.S.A. All rights reserved.
10 9 8 7 6 5 4 3 2 1

Library of Congress Cataloging-in-Publication Data
Wiseman, Bernard.
    Morris the moose.

    (An Early I can read book)
    Summary: Determined to prove that the cow he meets
is really a moose, Morris the moose enlists the help of
a rather confused deer and horse.
    [1. Moose—Fiction.   2. Animals—Fiction.
3. Humorous stories] I. Title. II. Series.
PZ7.W7802Mu 1989   [E]   87-33485
ISBN 0-06-026475-6
ISBN 0-06-026476-4 (lib. bdg.)

For Barbara Dicks

One day

Morris the Moose

saw a cow.

"You are

a funny-looking moose,"

he said.

"I am a COW.

I am not a MOOSE!"

said the cow.

"You have four legs

and a tail

and things on your head,"

said Morris.

"You are a moose."

7

"But I say MOO!"

said the cow.

"I can say MOO too!"

said Morris.

9

The cow said,

"I give MILK to people."

"So you are a moose

who gives milk to people!"

said Morris.

11

"But my mother

is a COW!"

said the cow.

"You are a MOOSE,"

said Morris.

"So your mother

must be a moose too!"

13

"What can I tell you?"

the cow said.

"You can tell me

you are a moose,"

said Morris.

14

"No!" cried the cow.

"I am NOT a moose!

Ask him.

He will tell you

what I am."

15

"What is she?"

Morris asked the deer.

The deer said,

"She has four legs

and a tail

and things on her head.

She is a deer, like me."

17

"She is a MOOSE, like ME!"

Morris yelled.

18

"You?

You are not a moose.

You are a deer too!"

The deer laughed.

"I am a MOOSE!"

cried Morris.

"You are a DEER!"

shouted the deer.

20

"What can I tell you?"

asked Morris.

"You can tell me

you are a deer,"

said the deer.

21

"Let's ask
somebody else,"
said the cow.

"Oh, dear." The cow sighed.

"Let's ask somebody else.

But first, let's get a drink."

"Okay, Moose," said Morris the Moose.

"Okay, Deer," said the deer.

23

They walked until

they found a horse.

"Hello, you horses!"

said the horse.

"What are those funny things

on your heads?"

Morris, the cow, and the deer

drank from a cool, blue stream.

Morris looked at himself

in the water and smiled.

"You two do not look

at all like me," he said.

"You cannot be moose."

"You mean,

you are not DEER,"

said the deer.

"You don't look

at all like me."

29

"See?" said the cow.

"I am not a moose

or a deer.

I am a COW!

You made a MISTAKE."

"I did not," said Morris.

"I made a MOOSEtake!"